Beauty &
THE BEAST

Beauty & THE BEAST

retold and illustrated by
MORDICAI GERSTEIN

E. P. Dutton   New York

Stories To Remember is produced by Joshua M. Greene
for Lightyear Entertainment, L.P.
350 Fifth Avenue, New York, New York 10118

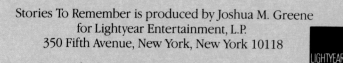

Copyright © 1989 Lightyear Entertainment, L.P.

Published in the United States
by E. P. Dutton, a division of Penguin Books USA Inc.
Published simultaneously in Canada
by Fitzhenry & Whiteside Limited, Toronto

Library of Congress Cataloging-in-Publication Data
Gerstein, Mordicai. Beauty & the beast / retold and illustrated by Mordicai Gerstein.—
1st ed. p. cm.
Summary: Through her great capacity to love, a kind and beautiful maid releases a
handsome prince from the spell which has made him an ugly beast.
ISBN 0-525-44510-2
(1. Fairy tales.   2. Folklore—France.)   I. Title.   II. Title: Beauty and the beast.
PZ8.G34Be   1989   398.21 0944—dc20   (E)
89-32194   CIP   AC

Designed by Antler & Baldwin Design Group

Printed in Colombia   ISBN: 0-525-44510-2
First Edition   10 9 8 7 6 5 4 3 2 1

For Susan

On a crisp fall morning, long, long ago, in a land that's now forgotten, a merchant whistled happily as he saddled his horse. He was off to meet a ship bringing him crates of precious ivory and Chinese silk.

"When I sell them, we shall be rich!" he told his daughters. "And I'll bring back gifts for each of you."

"A new gown, Father!" cried Edwina, his oldest. "I must have a new velvet gown!"

"She has gowns," whined Sybill, his middle daughter. "Bring me a gown, and a cape of green silk, and a hat covered with parrot feathers!"

"Enough!" cried their father. "You'll both have gowns and more." Then turning to his youngest, he said, "But you, Beauty, always so shy. What shall I bring for you?"

Beauty blushed and handed him his cloak. "There's nothing I really need, Father," she said. "Just come home quickly and safely."

"There must be something," insisted her father.

"Well," she said, "I'd love to have a rose, Father. If it's not too much trouble."

"What a ninny!" jeered her sisters. "She wants a rose!"

"A rose it will be," said the merchant. He waved good-bye and galloped off.

But when he got to the port, he learned that the ship had been wrecked in a storm. His ivory and silk lay at the bottom of the sea.

"I can't believe it," he said to himself. "I invested everything. Now I'm penniless." Stunned and empty-handed, he started for home.

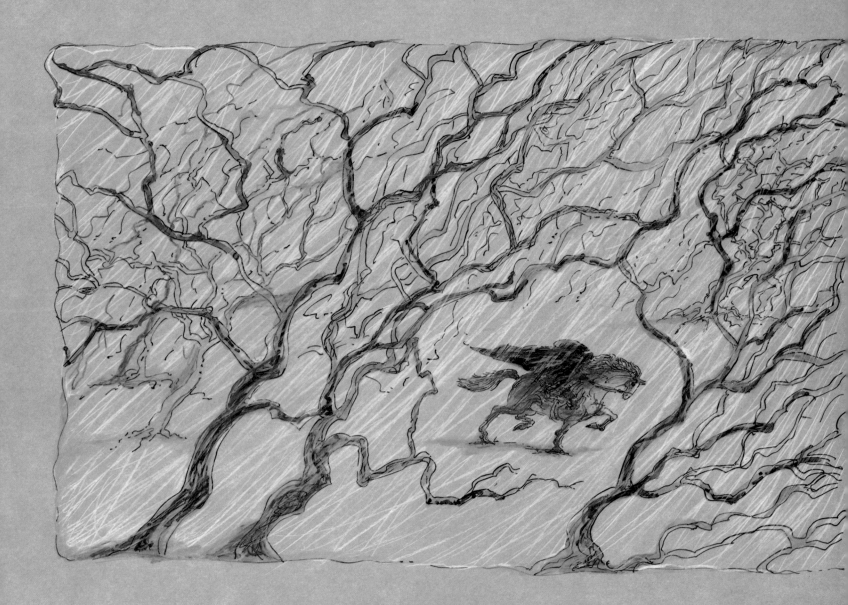

The day turned gray, and soon the air was full of snow. With evening, the snow became an icy sleet, and deep in the woods he realized he'd lost his way. The wind shrieked, the trees groaned, and when he heard the howls of wolves, the merchant thought himself as good as dead. Then, through the storm, he glimpsed a faint light. He spurred his horse toward it, fighting his way through the blinding sleet like a drowning man.

Suddenly the wind stopped. He looked around and found himself
in the peaceful warmth of a moonlit garden before a glowing palace.
Amazed, he left his horse and climbed slowly up the palace stairs. At the
top, massive doors of bronze swung silently open, and he stared into a
dazzling hall with marble floors like mirrors. Not a person was in sight.

"Hello! Hello!" called the merchant.

"Hello! *Hello*! Hello! *Hello*!" answered the echo, and then, except for the distant song of a nightingale, silence. The merchant went from room to room, each richer and stranger than the last. In a great dining hall, he found silver platters of steaming roasts, wine in crystal carafes, and rare fruit in golden baskets. The table was set for only one.

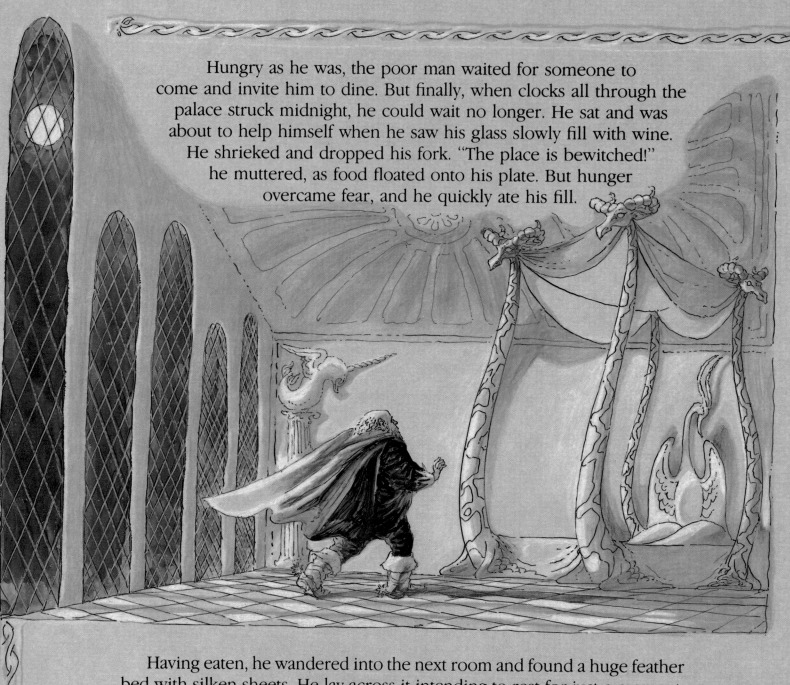

Hungry as he was, the poor man waited for someone to come and invite him to dine. But finally, when clocks all through the palace struck midnight, he could wait no longer. He sat and was about to help himself when he saw his glass slowly fill with wine. He shrieked and dropped his fork. "The place is bewitched!" he muttered, as food floated onto his plate. But hunger overcame fear, and he quickly ate his fill.

Having eaten, he wandered into the next room and found a huge feather bed with silken sheets. He lay across it intending to rest for just a moment, but fell into a deep sleep.

Sunlight woke him, and he was startled to find himself wearing a fine linen nightshirt and to see his clothes laid out, clean and dry. He dressed quickly and ran through the palace calling, "Who is master here?" But no one answered.

In the middle of a great empty ballroom, he stopped. Bowing low, he shouted, "Thank you, dear host! Thank you for saving my life and for your generous hospitality."

Outside, he was about to leave when he caught the scent of roses. He thought of his daughter, Beauty, and followed the scent through a maze of hedges.

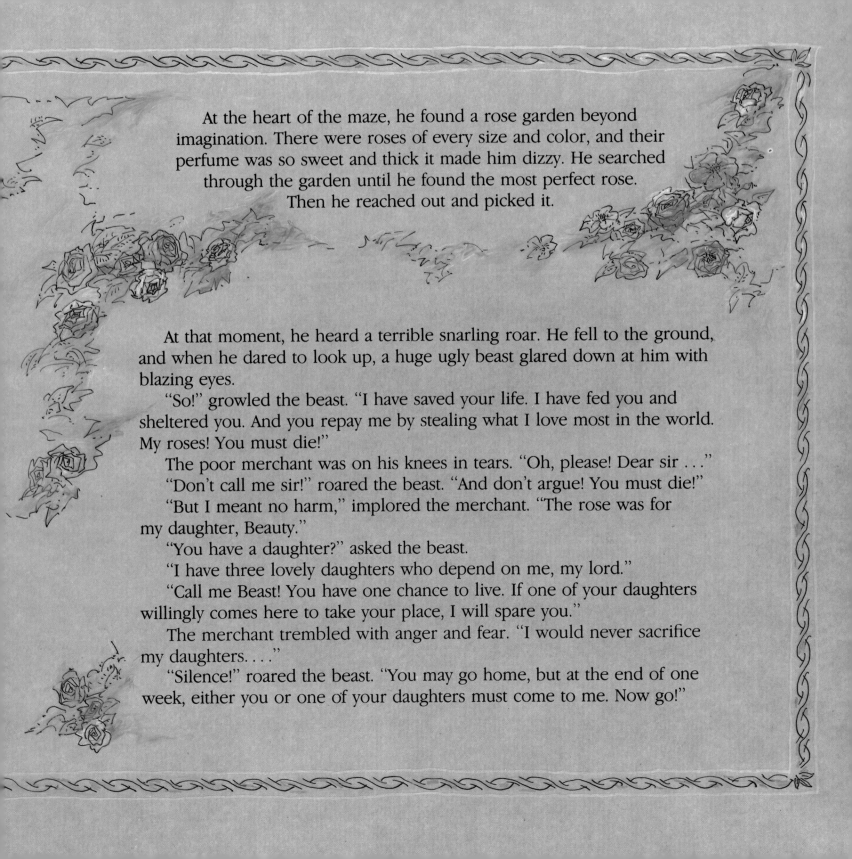

At the heart of the maze, he found a rose garden beyond imagination. There were roses of every size and color, and their perfume was so sweet and thick it made him dizzy. He searched through the garden until he found the most perfect rose. Then he reached out and picked it.

At that moment, he heard a terrible snarling roar. He fell to the ground, and when he dared to look up, a huge ugly beast glared down at him with blazing eyes.

"So!" growled the beast. "I have saved your life. I have fed you and sheltered you. And you repay me by stealing what I love most in the world. My roses! You must die!"

The poor merchant was on his knees in tears. "Oh, please! Dear sir ..."

"Don't call me sir!" roared the beast. "And don't argue! You must die!"

"But I meant no harm," implored the merchant. "The rose was for my daughter, Beauty."

"You have a daughter?" asked the beast.

"I have three lovely daughters who depend on me, my lord."

"Call me Beast! You have one chance to live. If one of your daughters willingly comes here to take your place, I will spare you."

The merchant trembled with anger and fear. "I would never sacrifice my daughters...."

"Silence!" roared the beast. "You may go home, but at the end of one week, either you or one of your daughters must come to me. Now go!"

At this, the merchant felt the garden spin around him, and he fainted dead away. When he opened his eyes, he was in his own bed, with Beauty holding his hand and her sisters looking down at him.

"Oh, Father!" said Beauty. "We're so glad you're alive! Your horse galloped into the yard last night, and you fell off unconscious. This was in your hand." She held up the rose, and the merchant began to weep, and he told them his story from start to finish.

"And so, in one week," he concluded, "I shall kiss you all good-bye for the last time."

Beauty burst into tears.

"But Father," wailed Sybill, "without you we'll starve!"

"It's all her fault!" snapped Edwina, pointing at Beauty. "She had to have a rose!"

"Yes!" cried Sybill. "She should go to the beast in your place, Father. He'd give her roses!"

"That's enough!" cried the merchant.

Beauty wept unconsolably. "They're right, Father," she sobbed. "They're right! Please forgive me!"

The week passed slowly. On the final
morning, Beauty was awakened at dawn by the clatter
of hooves. She ran out to the yard, and there stood a magnificent
white stallion with a golden saddle. She looked at the horse, and the
horse looked back at her and nodded. Her father peered out his window
just as Beauty leapt into the saddle.

"Beauty, no!" he shouted. "I forbid it!" But the stallion wheeled
around, jumped the fence, and disappeared into the morning mists. Her
father's cries were drowned out by the thudding hooves. Beauty laid her
cheek against the horse's neck. It was like riding the wind.

When the horse stopped, the mist cleared and there was the palace,
gleaming in the dewy sunlight. Beauty's heart was pounding as she went
up the steps. When the great bronze doors opened without a sound, she
cried out and covered her eyes. But when she peered between her
fingers, she saw no beast. She saw no one.

All through the silent palace she went, gazing in wonder at the strange rich rooms. Finally, on a door all covered with fantastic carvings, she watched as the words *Beauty's Room* appeared in letters of gold.

The room was full of sunlight, roses, and shelves of books. A book lying on the table slowly opened, and Beauty read,

Dearest Beauty, have no fear.
You alone are mistress here.
My palace, my gardens, my roses so sweet,
All that I have is laid at your feet.

"What does this mean?" cried Beauty, looking wildly around.

"What do you want of me?" But there was no answer.

Daylight faded into twilight, and all through the palace the candles lit themselves, one by one. In the great dining hall, Beauty sat alone and waited. The table was set with roses and silver and all her most favorite foods and cakes, but she touched nothing. Hours passed in eerie stillness. Then she noticed the smell of damp fur, and she heard the sound of breathing.

"Good evening, Beauty," growled a rasping voice.

When Beauty saw the beast, the earth seemed to drop from under her. She could never have imagined anything so monstrous.

"Good evening . . . sir," she stammered.

"Call me Beast! Did you come of your own choice, Beauty?"

"I did . . . Beast . . . to save my father," Beauty replied.

"And your room, does it please you?"

"It's lovely, Beast. Thank you."

"And Beauty, do you find me very ugly?"

Beauty faltered and looked down. Her heart pounded. "I cannot lie, Beast," she said at last. "I find you ugly."

"Yes," sighed the beast. "I am ugly." He shut his eyes for a moment, and then jumped up and struck the table.

"I am ugly!" he roared. "And I am a beast!" He glared at her. Then he covered his eyes, and after a moment said softly, "Beauty, may I sit with you each evening while you dine?"

"If you wish," said Beauty.

"And Beauty," he said, in a rasping whisper, "will you be my wife?"

Beauty looked down and saw her hands trembling. She closed her eyes. It was several moments before she could look up and say, "I cannot, Beast. I do not love you."

The beast groaned and turned away.

"Good night, Beauty," he said.

She watched him go slowly down the hall. Then she collapsed weeping at the table.

Beauty dreamt that night of a nightingale that flew in her window and perched on her bed. The bird sang a sweet, haunting song:

Dearest Beauty, have no fear.
You alone are mistress here.
Trust your heart and not your eyes.
Appearances are full of lies.

Sunlight woke her. She dressed and wandered out among roses of every color and fragrance. She saw exotic flowers she never dreamed existed. She came upon a huge cage full of strange and wondrous birds. They looked at her and fluttered helplessly against the bars.

"I wish I could free you," she said. Then she thought of the beast and shuddered.

Each evening, he sat opposite her and asked about her day and watched her every move.

"His eyes," she thought, "are not the eyes of a beast. They're so sad and full of mysteries."

One night, feeling bold, she asked him, "Beast, when will you kill me?"

Beauty saw him flinch, and his eyes filled with horror.

"Don't you know, Beauty," he said, "I would never harm you in any way." Then, covering his face, he said, "Please forgive me," and quickly left the room.

The next evening, as she waited for the beast to appear, there was a sudden flutter of wings, and a bird flew around and around the room. Then she saw the beast in the doorway, and quick as any cat, his arm shot out and the bird was in his fist. Beauty could see it looking out at her from between his claws. It was a nightingale.

"Oh, please," she said. "Let it go."

The beast stood perfectly still and looked at her. Slowly his hand opened, and the bird flew out the window into the night, singing.

"Beast," said Beauty, "when will you set *me* free?" She looked again into his eyes, and it was like looking into a forest: Behind a tree she saw a fox, here the flash of some bird, there a young fawn.

"Beauty," he said softly, "will you be my wife?"

"Dear Beast," she heard herself say, "you know I cannot."

She dreamed that night that she rode on the back of a wolf in the arms of a handsome stranger, a prince, through a fantastic forest of vines and flowers. Ahead of them flew the nightingale. Then she heard her father calling her, "Beauty! Beauty!" with his voice growing fainter and fainter.

She woke and realized that it had been weeks since she had thought of him.

"Oh, Father!" she said aloud. "If only I could see you!"

She glanced into the mirror by her bed, and there she saw her father. He looked old and sick. His lips moved, speaking her name. She burst into tears, and that evening when the beast appeared, she fell to her knees and said, "Please, Beast! Let me go to my father. I'm afraid he is dying."

The beast raised her to her feet. "I am only a beast," he said, "but I would die if you left me, Beauty."

"Oh, just for one week," said Beauty. "He needs me, and I miss him so."

The beast did not answer. He watched her for a long while, and at last he asked, "Beauty, will you be my wife?"

She did not look at him. "Dear gentle Beast," she said, "I cannot."

She was awakened that night by mournful howls and the sound of something crashing through the woods. She left her bed and hurried through the moonlit maze until she stood in the rose garden. The beast stepped out of the black shadows. His fur was torn and wild, and the moon trembled in his eyes.

"Beauty," he said, "you may go to your father for one week, but if you stay away longer, I will surely die. Take this ring. Leave it on your table, and you will wake in your father's house."

"Oh, thank you, dear Beast! Thank you!" She took the beast's hand and kissed it, and smelled the forest. She felt the coarse fur and the sharp claws.

"I am ugly," he said. "I am a beast and a fool. But, Beauty, my heart is good."

She looked into his eyes and almost wept. She saw such pain.

"Beauty," he whispered, "will you be my wife?"

"Dearest Beast," she answered, but looked away and shook her head.

Returning to her room, she put the ring on her table, and when she awoke, she was indeed in her father's house. She jumped out of bed and ran to his room.

"Beauty!" he cried. "You're alive!" He embraced her and kissed her again and again. "Dear Beauty, you will make me well!"

When she looked around, she saw that the house was now richly furnished and handsome.

"The morning you left," said her father, "I found this chest of gold on the doorstep, and no matter how much I spend, it's never empty."

"And my sisters?" asked Beauty. "How are they?"

"Thanks to the gold," sighed her father, "they're both married now. I'll send for them."

Edwina had married a handsome man who was vain and stupid, and
Sybill had married a sly man who was mean and petty. The sisters were
both miserable, and secretly hoped that Beauty had been torn to shreds
by the beast. When they saw her, radiant and looking like a princess, it
was all they could do to hide their jealousy and rage.

"Oh, we've missed you so!" they said, as they embraced her.

"And I've missed you," said Beauty, "but I can only stay one week. The beast said he would die if I didn't return."

"The evil thing!" said Edwina. "Let him die!"

"Yes!" cried Sybill. "Then his palace would be ours!"

"And of course," added Edwina, "you would be free."

Beauty shook her head. "He's been kind to me," she said. "And I promised."

Her sisters stared at her. "You must be mad!" they said.

Later, Edwina drew Sybill aside and whispered, "She wants all the wealth for herself, the greedy pig!"

"Yes!" said Sybill. "Let's keep her here beyond the week. Either the beast will die, or he'll tear her limb from limb for being late."

"Perfect!" said Edwina. So, when the time came for Beauty to leave, her sisters rubbed their eyes with onion, and tears flowed.

"Oh, please stay!" blubbered Edwina.

"Please!" sobbed Sybill. "For Father's sake."

Beauty smelled the onion and doubted her sisters' tears. But her father had recovered, and he wept too. She found herself staying another day, and then another, until the beast and his palace began to seem unreal, like some children's fairy tale.

After ten days, she had a dream. She was alone at the beast's table, but it was dark and cold. From far off she heard a pitiful groaning.

"Beast, is that you?" she asked, getting to her feet.

"Beast! Answer me!" she cried, running through the palace.

"Forgive me for staying away so long!" she pleaded, now running through the gardens. But she heard the groans growing weaker and weaker.

"Don't die, Beast!" cried Beauty, running frantically through the moonlit maze. Then she heard the nightingale singing:

Dearest Beauty, the hour is late.
Happiness won't always wait.
Run to the center of your own heart's maze.
There find love for all your days.

Beauty woke with tears streaming down her face. She put the beast's ring on her table and fell back asleep. When she woke again, she was in the beast's palace. She ran to the center of the maze. There in the rose garden the beast lay sprawled in the moonlight, limp and motionless.

"Oh, dearest Beast!" cried Beauty. "Please live. Please live and marry me, and I'll never leave you again. I love you."

At these words, the sun rose and the great bird cage in the garden burst open, and the air was full of birds and their rejoicing. But Beauty barely noticed, for the beast had opened his eyes and looked at her. And as she watched his face, he was transformed into a young and handsome prince.

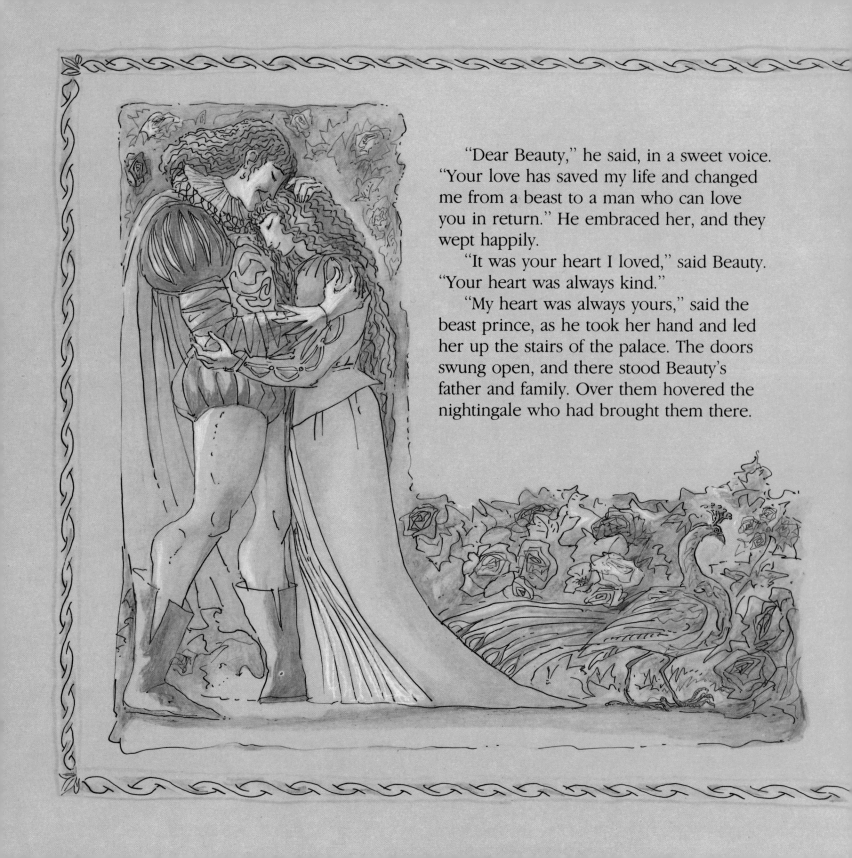

"Dear Beauty," he said, in a sweet voice. "Your love has saved my life and changed me from a beast to a man who can love you in return." He embraced her, and they wept happily.

"It was your heart I loved," said Beauty. "Your heart was always kind."

"My heart was always yours," said the beast prince, as he took her hand and led her up the stairs of the palace. The doors swung open, and there stood Beauty's father and family. Over them hovered the nightingale who had brought them there.

The nightingale sang:

Dearest Beauty, full of grace,
Your heart's as lovely as your face.
You freed the Prince, transformed the beast,
Now all may dance at your wedding feast.

They were married that very day.
Everyone laughed and cried. Everyone, that is,
except the sisters, who were rigid with
jealousy and rage.

"Dear sisters," said Beauty, "give up
your jealousy and hate. Open your hearts and
my happiness can be your own."

But the sisters refused, and in moments, beginning with their hearts, they turned to stone. They became two statues at the doors of the palace. There they stood through the years and watched as Beauty and the Prince filled the palace with laughter, children, and roses.

The Prince and Beauty lived long and happily, and their story lives after them. And it always will, as long as there is someone to tell it and someone to listen.